D0930539

for P5 and P6
of St. Mary's Girls School
who paid me a visit

M.W.

First published in the United States in 1988 by E. P. Dutton,
2 Park Avenue, New York, N.Y. 10016,
a division of NAL Penguin Inc.
Originally published in Great Britain in 1988
by Methuen Children's Books Ltd,
11 New Fetter Lane, London EC4P 4EE
Printed in Spain OBE First American Edition
ISBN: 0-525-44385-1 10 9 8 7 6 5 4 3 2 1

by Martin Waddell
pictures by
Jonathan Langley

E. P. DUTTON NEW YORK

Alice is an artist.

One day she had an idea for a picture.

When the picture was finished,
Alice stepped back to look at it.

“I like it!” said Alice.

“It would be better with an elephant in it,” said Alice’s friend, Alfred.

So Alice added Alfred's elephant.

"Give it an umbrella," said Amanda.
"A frilly one, like mine."

So Alice added Amanda's umbrella.

“What your picture needs is my bicycle!” suggested Betty.

So Alice added Betty's bicycle.

"Fill it up with my flowers!"
said Frankie.

So Alice added Frankie's flowers.

"My bees would brighten it up!" said Bertie.

So Alice added Bertie's bees.

"Put in my tiger!" said Terry.
"It'll make it more exciting!"

So Alice added Terry's tiger.

"Finished!" said Alice, proudly.
"What do you think of my picture?"
But nobody was left, except the tiger.

The tiger roared at her and ate the picture.

"Oh dear," said Alice. "Didn't you like it?"

"It tasted rotten!" said the tiger,
and he went away.

“I’ve got an idea!” shouted Alice.

“I’m doing it my own way, this time!”

“I like it!” said Alice.